Someone Gets To Love Him

LK WOLLETT

Published by LK WOLLETT, 2023.

SOMEONE GETS TO LOVE HIM

First edition. September 16, 2023.

ISBN: 979-8223563150

Written by LK WOLLETT.

Someone Gets to Love Him

With bonus: "In His Presence"
By LK Wollett

Chapter 1

You would have thought the King or some Hollywood star was expected with all the activity in the hall. Furniture was being carried out of the corner office; the one with floor to ceiling windows and sculpted mahogany paneling. Then carpet cleaners went in. The next day, the new desk with matching cadenza, conference table, bookcase and file cabinet along with ergonomic chair arrived followed by computer monitors. Not everyone got to witness this activity because they sat in offices. I, Shelly, worked in an area of secured, original hard copy files where I stood most of the time so I could see everything.

With filing done for the day and files locked securely, I stopped by Annie's office to say 'good-night'. I also mentioned the new furniture in the corner office and, because she was assistant to the new executive moving in, she gave me a tour. Though she knew the man's name, Robert Burns, she didn't know where he was from or if he had family. She would know soon enough though because she tended to be used as assistant to the wife.

Getting home to my mom's trailer later that afternoon, Mom was making dinner and I love her cooking, eating more than I should then try to exercise it off. Dad passed away a few years ago leaving her financially stable and, though I worked a full time job in a factory when I first moved in with her, she didn't like that I was gone before she woke up and home after she went to bed. I also didn't like my job, which she perceived, I guess. For many months, she hinted that she would love my company during the day and I could quit. When Annie, who I knew from church, spoke of the part-time filing job, I thought that was a good option.

Anyway, it was a few days before I got a look at Mr. Burns and then it was only the back of his head and shoulders. In a tailored dark navy suit jacket with golden brown hair, medium cut, I liked what I saw. Annie was busy walking in and out of his office and I could hear him talking though not understanding his words, along with frequent soft laughter. A group of executives then went into his office shutting his door and it was shut when I left for the day.

On my next office day, Mr. Burns' office was dark; Annie said he was out of the country. He was becoming a mystery to me that needed to be solved. Where was he from? Was he married? You know, all those 'get-acquainted' questions? Annie was no help. She said she had not met a wife and he did not share personal information. Neither did he ask personal questions. It's not that he was rude or offensive; he was cordial and focused on his work.

Finally, I got to see his face, even though it was a picture in the company bulletin. His eyes stood out to me first, intense blue, looking at me directly. Then his smile: natural, genuine, set off by his tailored black suit with white shirt and current-style tie. In another picture continued on the next page, he was not smiling and a distinct dimple in his chin became clear. It looked like he was intensely focused on the object of his attention or the thought in his head with a steady determination. Studying the picture I thought, longingly, 'someone gets to love this man'.

Seven years ago, or maybe eight now, I was married in a beautiful wedding ceremony, and lived in the typical suburban home, but the relationship fell apart for several reasons.

Honesty. Though my husband, Todd, said he loved me and would never leave me, he also wanted a family. I did too but my body wouldn't produce a baby and doctors could not make it happen with the resources we had. Todd eventually agreed to visit adoption agencies but the process was offensive to him. Though I could see myself living with a number of the orphans, he could not. So he, honestly, wanted me for a family and I alone was not enough for him. His disappointment could not be overcome and we agreed to part.

Self versus Other. If Todd could have focused on the needs of the orphans, adoption would have been easy. He chose however to focus on fulfilling his vision of a family. Enough said.

Trust. This had nothing to do with Todd. I know now that I hid part of myself from him, and I probably would have with any man, because I was afraid I wasn't good enough; I was afraid of what he would think of me. Most of the day, this didn't matter; it mattered during intimacy. What I did with him then was scripted and, I'll be honest, tiring for me. I think the common description of me would be 'cold'.

Awareness. I didn't treasure Todd. Today, if I could have Todd back again, he would be gold to me. That won't happen though because he found a nice girl who is giving him babies.

For some, this may be uncomfortable or maybe confusing but I believe awareness I have now is because of Jesus. Though Todd did not attend church and I quit after we were married, I went to church many years of my life. In my despair at losing Todd, I cried out to God and he awakened my spirit; in other words, I was 'born-again'[1]. The Bible calls salvation a 'free gift'[2] and believe me, gifts abound when your spirit is awakened. The gift I am referring to now is love of others; it is a love that is poured into you by the Holy Spirit[3]. And when the object of this love is your spouse, given to you by God, it is intensified[4].

Chapter 2

Finally, Mr. Burns returned to his office and, as I was filing, I could hear him talking to Annie and others, never understanding the sentences, which wasn't my business anyway. Suddenly, a piercing, obnoxious horn blared over the announcement system followed by a command to shelter in place. Annie popped into my cubicle to show me the way, saying it was a tornado warning. Stepping into a door that led to a short hallway, we entered a lunch room with kitchenette and tables. Annie and I sat down; she texted her husband. Mr. Burns and another younger man, Mike, followed, both with laptops.

"Annie," Mr. Burns said gently and she moved across from him. "My three o'clock flight; I won't make it if this lasts long."

"Let's see," she said concentrating on her computer tablet, "A five o'clock will arrive at seven, with one stop. I don't see any directs."

"Let's do the five o'clock and cancel dinner with Fred," Mr. Burns answered. "See if he can meet for breakfast."

Watching him talk to Annie, look at his laptop, talk to Mike, smiling occasionally, I wanted to dismiss both of them and climb onto his lap so he would talk to me. But if he noticed me, he gave no indication. Suddenly everyone's head jerked upward when a wind gust rattled the roof then the walls started shaking. Lights went out; then dim emergency lights came on. Mr. Burns yelled 'GET DOWN!' and ducked under the table followed by the rest of us. Annie reached for me to come closer and, as I reached for her, the table lifted off of us crashing into the wall; kitchen cabinets were being pulled out of place with the doors swinging wildly. Everything in the cabinets crashed to the floor. Instinctively, I curled into a ball with my arms covering my head, my back to the wind; my body was being pushed in jerks along the wet floor. Debris, small pellets and large pieces of wood and cardboard, pummeled my body. As I trembled uncontrollably, I asked God to help me; to help us. Knowing Annie was ready to meet Jesus, I added my concern for the two men. Then a sharp cry leapt out of Annie. Looking in her direction, she was wailing and sobbing, and an iron rod, maybe a foot long, protruded from her right shoulder. Blood was seeping but not gushing.

Seconds later, the wind stopped and Mr. Burns swept Annie into his arms sprinting toward the road, dodging debris like a running back dodging tackles. Though Mike and I rushed after him, he was yards ahead, heading for the hospital. We stopped following when a car picked them up. Sirens and security alarms blared everywhere. Other people from the office emerged from the building.

The roof on front of the office building was pealed back like the lid of a vegetable can. Floor to ceiling windows in Mr. Burn's office were gone; the sculpted mahogany wall between his office and the kitchen was gone along with the matching furniture. The files where I worked were standing and undamaged; I was told they were built and installed to withstand disaster. A giant tree covered my car along with other cars but not Mike's. Expressing concern about my mom, Mike asked the security people if we could go.

It took a lot of slow maneuvering and several stops to remove debris in the road before we got home. Mom rushed out of the trailer to embrace me, wailing that she had tried to call my cell and the office. Thankfully, the tornado's path did not come near her. Mom asked Mike about his family and he said he lived in another state; he had traveled here to meet with Mr. Burns. Mom walked toward the trailer inviting him to come in. She was cooking and I was so glad.

Mom told us to wash up and change our clothes because my backside was covered with dirt; Mike's backside as well. He still couldn't get cell coverage to check with the hotel or call his parents. As I went into the bathroom, Mom put a blanket on Dad's easy chair for Mike and handed him the TV remote. She thought she could find something of Dad's he could wear.

When I came into the living room dressed, Mike was watching the devastation on the news. Mom handed him some sweats and a tee shirt with towels and wash cloth and led him to the bathroom. As I watched the news report, I jumped out of my skin when my phone rang. It was Annie's husband, Doug.

"Are you alright?" Doug exclaimed.

"Yes, yes!" I blurted. "What about Annie?"

"She's resting. They got it out." Doug said emotionally, letting a sob loose. "It missed her bones, thank God. She asked about you first thing."

"Please tell her I'm fine and I'm home. Mom is fine." I responded. "Did you see Mr. Burns?"

"He was gone when I got here," Doug replied. "But I'll thank God for him as long as I live."

Mike emerged from the bathroom giving Dad's tee shirt and sweats a completely different look, a look any Stud would admire. With his suit, briefs, shoes and socks in his hands, he asked Mom if the suit could be cleaned and she told him to take it out to the water hose to get off as much dirt as possible. To help Mom, I went into the bathroom to straighten up, freshen towels if needed, and was greeted by the seat up on the toilet. In my married life, I would have been annoyed. Women are supposed to be annoyed by this, right? Now, I would pay a fortune to have it back in my life.

Mom was putting food on the table when I walked back to her. Mike was hanging the suit on the porch. Asking what he should do with his briefs, shoes and socks, she handed him a trash bag saying he could put the suit in it when it was dry. He left the trash bag on the porch.

At the table, Mom and I bowed our heads which caught Mike off guard. While eating, Mom found out where Mike was from and he was single, in his early twenties, had a masters in business and was a recently-hired manager for one of the company's branches. Mr. Burns was training him. Though he didn't have to live with his parents, he chose to do so because they were having health issues. He said he was finally able to call them on his cell and also the hotel, which had no power. Hearing that, Mom invited him to sleep here and he accepted.

As I helped Mom clean the kitchen, Mike watched the news. Then, as I usually did, to work off Mom's delicious food, I announced I was taking a walk; Mike came with me. Though I walked briskly, he wanted to run and challenged me to join him. He was in his bare feet, mind you. When I declined, he took off then came back; I think he forgot he wasn't wearing briefs as he jogged in place in front of me, challenging me again. He made me laugh then he took off. This time he ran out of my sight and I reached the place where I usually turn around; the sun was hitting the horizon. Waiting until I saw him, I turned to walk home. He ran passed me. I'm not sure what was holding up his sweats; I could see the top of his young, solid butt. Was he doing this on purpose? He didn't come back to me this time; he was sitting on the porch steps and he had worked up a sweat. Not sure if he was making advances toward me, I brushed passed him like he wasn't there.

It was passed Mom's bedtime when she went into her room. Telling Mike to help himself to anything in the fridge or pantry, he started asking me 'get-acquainted' questions. As I remained standing I told him I was soon to be thirty, divorced, no children, with a high school education and he knew the rest. Asking questions about the divorce, I gave him a quick version of my reasons and added that it led me to Jesus so, in the end, it was a positive outcome for me. With that, he murmured something about his sister going through a divorce, and the conversation was over. I wished him a good-night.

The next morning, I went into the bathroom, where the toilet seat was up, and Mom was asking Mike if he wanted coffee. He was watching the news in Dad's easy chair. He said he would take black and she brought him a cup. Then asking him if he wanted eggs and bacon, he said he did. When she told me she didn't need help, I got a cup of coffee and sat at the kitchen table. My insurance agent called and I'm so glad she did because I had forgotten about my car. I told her where it was and she said they would call me back. Mom put plates of eggs and bacon on the table and called Mike. As he walked toward me, I could see the hairline of his groin and could not stop a smile. Was he really this careless or just a show-off?

"I see Dad's sweats are too big for you," I hinted.

"You think so?" he challenged, looking down then pulling them up a little, ignoring the string.

"Have you ever modeled for one of those show-off calendars?" I teased.

"Show-off?" he questioned as he took his seat.

"Where the guys show-off what they have for charity," I explained.

"Never been invited but I suppose I could," Mike answered with an impish smile. "It would probably be a fun gig."

"Jesus would call that fornication," Mom stated, not looking up.

"Thank you, Mom," I thought to myself, gratefully.

"It's just a little fun, isn't it," Mike responded. "Who is hurt?"

"Anyone who don't follow Jesus are hurt, Son," Mom declared. "People who follow Jesus don't fornicate[5]. People who don't follow Jesus are hurt on Judgment Day when they are escorted to the burning lake of fire[6]. There's some 'hurt' for you."

Conversation died at that moment, and my phone rang with the news that my car was totaled and was being towed. Mike left the table with his breakfast half eaten and grabbed the trash bag. When he emerged from the bathroom, the string on his sweats was pulled tight. He put his suit into the trash bag then walked to the table saying he should leave. Though I thought about asking him for a ride to my car, I decided it would be best to give him space. He just got a dose of the truth and he was experiencing the side-effects.

Chapter 3

Two months after the tornado, I asked Annie why I had not been called back to work. She didn't know and suggested I call Personnel. They said the position had been eliminated and, in the chaos, they had not yet sent out a notice. So, thinking that door was closed for whatever reason, I looked to God for the next opening or path. Mom and I stayed active with various church activities, deciding for the first time to travel to a church conference at a hotel on the Gulf Coast. As we stood at a hotel counter to check in, I heard Mr. Burns. Turning to see him, he was walking in with a stunning group of people. Three men, in dark suits, white shirts and current style ties, were about the same height and the heads of the adult women, in slim skirts with matching jackets, came to their shoulders. The young people looked like shorter versions of the adults. You would have to use the adjectives 'poise','sophistication', and 'wealth' to describe them. The hotel clerk asked for my credit card so I turned to her. When I looked back, Mr. Burns and his group were gone.

After Mom and I got settled in our room, we found the location of the church conference. Praise and worship music poured over the speakers as images flashed across a giant screen. Neither Mom or I had ever been to a live concert so we were mesmerized by the lights and cameras. After some announcements were made, the first speaker, who Mom and I had heard many times on TV, came to the microphone. When all the speakers were done, we found a restaurant for supper then headed to our room. Our plan was to spend the night and head to the airport in the morning. Both of us were tired but very pleased we attended.

Around midnight, a siren went off then someone was pounding furiously on the door bellowing they were Security. I ran to the door and they said we had to evacuate. Running into get Mom, neither of us had robes or slippers so I grabbed a sheet and our purses. The security man said there was a bomb scare and we were going to a shelter. Not using the elevators, we descended the stairs several flights to the ground floor, walked past the conference room we were in earlier, into a courtyard and into a different building where we interrupted a wedding party. Available chairs were taken so Mom and I found an alcove where she could sit on the edge of a stone enclosure of a large tree. Mom had on sweats and a tee shirt; I was wrapped in a sheet because my sleepwear was designed to show off what I had, not cover it. Both of us were bare foot.

People coming into the room were bringing cool air with them so I sat close to mom, not looking around. A pair of long legs in black tuxedo pants and shiny leather shoes passed and sat in the vacant spot beside me.

"Shelly?" said Mr. Burns. "Are you alright?"

Looking up at him in wonder that he was sitting next to me with his strong arm touching my shoulder, that he was speaking to me and that he knew my name, I nodded that I was alright.

"I think the disasters are following me," I quipped.

He leaned back and a deep laugh escaped from his wide smile. Before more words could be said, a dainty six-year old girl with golden blond curls in a lavish pink lace party dress jumped on his lap.

"OOOFFF!" came out of Mr. Burns as he cupped his arms around her in a protective manner.

She squealed at the noise he made and bounced on him again.

"OOOFFF! OOOFFF!" escaped two more times as she bounced on him.

A woman rushed up to the little girl to retrieve her.

"Mandy," the woman said as she walked away. "You'll hurt Uncle Rob."

Mr. Burns watched them for a few seconds with a smile then turned to me like the incident never occurred.

"They could be following me, you know," he replied looking right at me with a reassuring smile. "The disasters, I mean."

"You're with the wedding?" my precious mom asked with no shyness.

"This is my Mom, Betty," I interjected.

"Rob Burns, Betty," he greeted. "Best man for my brother."

"What you did for Annie was a miracle, I'd say," Mom declared.

"That's what military does for you," Rob answered humbly. "She was injured and I took her to where she needed to go."

"Military?" Mom prompted.

"Only two years hard core," he replied. "Never deployed but lots of war games, drills...then I went into reserve. Still there."

"There's Mike!" I interrupted, seeing him walk our way with a smile.

"We're heading out," Mike stated, leaning close to Rob; ignoring my mom and me.

"OK, see you tomorrow," Rob replied and Rob stood to embrace him for a second, patting his back robustly.

"Your son?" Mom pried.

"Mom, Rob isn't old enough..." I exclaimed with embarrassment.

"An associate," Rob chuckled. "He told me you put him up that night."

"He's got some ornery in him," my mom announced. "It'll get him in trouble if he ain't watched. He needs some Jesus."

I don't know if Rob heard my mom because a young woman, shoulder-length, blond hair, black shiny tank top showing off sculpted, tan arms, in black tailored pants, rushed up to Rob to say they were leaving and wasn't he coming. With jokes and giggles between each sentence, she explained where they were going and asked again if he was coming. He listened intently, responding when he needed to respond and he said her name a couple of times, Lori. Getting up like he was going to leave with the young woman, I smiled to myself when he asked if we wanted anything. Coffee? Water? Both of us said water. I watched him move through the crowd stopping often to speak or listen. He disappeared completely and was gone several minutes. When he returned with bottles of water, he said we should be going to our room in moments. Looking over the crowd now, very few wedding guests were left and I dared to wonder if he was staying behind because of me. But it was probably because he was a decent, caring person.

"You shook him up, Betty," Rob revealed, continuing the conversation. "He said you are religious."

"Not religious," Mom corrected. "Pharisees were religious. We follow Jesus with our prayers and Bible study. We got a good church over on Parsons Road anytime you want to go."

Looking at my mom with admiration, I often prayed to be outspoken like her. When I asked her how she did it, she said it came with age and not fearing what people thought of her. Security then announced the hotel was clear and we rose to follow the crowd. Rob escorted us to our room then stopped outside the door to say 'good night'. He turned toward the elevator not looking back but I closed the door slowly watching him through a slim crack while I let the sheet slide off my back.

Chapter 4

Not long after our trip, I received notice that the filing job was available and happily returned to the company. With some admonitions from Mom about being yoked to an unbeliever[7], I did pray for God's guidance and wisdom. The office had been moved to Downtown, next to state and federal government offices with no glass windows anywhere.

Like before, the files were located close to Mr. Burns, now Rob, and, like before, I could hear him talking to Annie and various people but now I could picture what facial expressions and gestures might be accompanying his tone. Sometimes, Lori, who had now joined the company, would talk to him - she was the young woman who made lots of jokes and giggles between sentences. Then I would make a reason to walk into the hallway to see what she was wearing, which was always tasteful, cute, current...everything I wasn't, in other words. Why did I torture myself?

Almost a year passed with me filing and turning thirty; Annie having a baby; and no apparent change in Rob's life. It was evident he had no wife or children unless you want to call his work 'his wife'. Annie mentioned a few times Rob's devotion to his family and how he prioritized his time to be with them no matter where they were. Annie wasn't sure if Lori was related.

One afternoon as closing time approached, we were told downtown roads were closed because of a peaceful protest occurring at one of the government offices. I called my mom and she said she was watching the news. Sitting with Annie in her office, we also watched the news on her computer tablet and the crowd was massive. From a helicopter view, we could see our building was surrounded by protestors. As Annie and I chatted quietly about her baby and she showed me pictures, the news showed some fights breaking out in the crowd. Although SWAT officers quickly surrounded the outbreak, protestors started fighting with police and the escalation began. Even though Annie's office was not on an outer wall, we could hear thumps, breaking glass and shouting. The news showed flames leaping out of a few stores connected to our building. Fire trucks rolled toward the crowd blasting them with water. Rob appeared in the hall sprinting toward us.

"Get your things!" he blurted as he ran into his office, reappearing in seconds with a laptop bag. "Come with me!"

Annie stuffed her laptop bag and grabbed her purse; I grabbed mine. Both of us squealed as the overhead sprinklers came on. A couple other people stood with us waiting on Rob who was checking every office on the floor, yelling at people to go to the stairs. When he was satisfied that the floor was empty, he led us to several flights of stairs and we eventually stepped onto the roof. Security led us to an area beside a helicopter pad. Rob went back into the building. When a helicopter landed to take people, I stepped to the back of the group because I wanted to ride with Rob. Annie looked at me as she approached the helicopter and I waved her on. I prayed for God to help us; to help Rob.

After ten minutes, maybe more, Rob did not reappear. As the sun was setting and the security people were watching the chaos, I slipped back into the building. Entering the floor that the steps led to, I rushed through a door calling Rob's name. Black smoke hung down from the ceiling. When no-one answered, I rushed to the next floor, entered a door then called, and then rushed to the next floor and entered a door where it was pitch black and the black smoke was just above my head.

"Rob!" I shouted.

"Shelly?" Rob answered then he said quickly. "Stay where you are; say my name again."

"Rob!" I shouted as tears wet my face; I wanted to run to him. "ROB!"

As I heard movement, I looked in its direction.

"ROB!" I repeated, hysterically sobbing.

"Stay where you are, Shelly!" he warned. "Stay next to the door!"

I did as he commanded and I could hear movement.

"I'm ok, Shelly," he reassured. "I'm almost there. Say my name again."

"MR. BURNS!" I yelled which made him chuckle; I thought it would. "THIS WAY!"

Finally, his head practically bumped into my leg; he had been crawling. I knelt down and he sat back on his legs. His intense blue eyes were looking in my direction although I didn't know if he saw me. His face was neutral.

"Feel the door," he said quietly. "If it's cool to the touch, we can go out. If it's hot, we might be in trouble."

"It's cool," I said.

He rose and took my hand to help me up. We met a security officer in the stairwell who asked if we needed help. Telling him we were OK, we ascended stairs then stepped onto the roof and into the waiting helicopter. Ten or so other people were seated with us. Though Rob sat beside me, he remained quiet, thoughtful.

"Mr. Burns?" he finally asked, turning his head toward me for a second then it tilted back as a burst of laughter escaped. "You're standing in a burning building and you decide to make a joke?"

He turned his body toward me with wonder on his face.

"That was awesome," he stated, nodding his head.

The helicopter landed at the airport and we were taken into a building where police were taking information and medics were checking for injuries. Though I said I was fine, Rob let them take vitals and check his eyes. Wanting to give them space, I walked to a table to get a coffee. I found a seat, called my mom and she was relieved to hear from me. She said the protestors had been disbanded and firemen were soaking the smoldering buildings. My building was one of them. When I ended the call, whatever was holding me up let me go and I laid back, closing my eyes, with no energy.

"Are you sure you're alright?" Rob asked with concern as he sat beside me.

"I'm coming down from the adrenaline high," I explained. "I will be glad to get home. Are you alright?"

"Some smoke inhalation," he answered, "which I expected. It will clear up. Maneuvering in smoke is one of the military drills but I failed this exercise."

"What happened?" I asked, sitting up with interest.

"I got disoriented and couldn't find the door," he explained then he mused. "I shouldn't have gone in there alone. You won't let me do that again, will you?"

I promised him and I wished with all my heart that I would always be with him so I could keep the promise.

"I'm renting a van," he stated, "to take people home. Need a ride?"

As he rose, I followed him through the group of people as he offered people rides. I called my mom to tell her we were leaving the airport. With nine people in the van, we made six stops and my trailer was last so I was sitting in the front seat with him. When we pulled into the drive, he rushed out to open my door. Mom burst out of the house to embrace me and she expressed gratitude to Rob for bringing me home safe. Inviting him to come in, he said he was going back to the airport but he followed us to the door. As he said 'good-night' and walked away, I watched him; this time he looked back at me with a smile and waved.

"That's progress," I thought.

Chapter 5

As the company was relocated again, Mom and I again stayed busy with church activities and occasionally we watched Annie's baby, Chrissy, going on two years old and, because Annie was due for another baby, she invited Mom and me to a Gender Reveal party. To my delight, Rob was standing in the large back yard being introduced to Annie's friends and relatives. She saw Mom and me, got us a beverage and we found a seat at one of the tables where I watched Rob make an effort to greet and engage, if possible, every one of the thirty or so people.

We must have been one of the last to arrive, because, with much excitement, Doug, Annie and Chrissy opened a giant box releasing several pink balloons. Annie invited all of us to get a plate of food then Mom and I returned to our seat. Rob came out of the house with his plate and I smiled automatically as he headed our way.

"Ladies," he greeted and we nodded. "How have you been?"

"Blessed we are," Mom answered and I followed with an 'amen'.

"So you're not religious like the Pharisees, you said," Rob continued from a conversation over a year ago. "I was wondering what made the Pharisees religious."

"They followed Moses' law to show people they were superior," Mom answered.

"But if they followed the law, weren't they superior?" Rob asked.

"They should have followed it to please God, but they were focused on themselves," Mom began. "There's a wealth of knowledge in the Bible, Son, but one thing you got to know: 'God needed a perfect sacrifice to save his creation and Jesus provided that perfect sacrifice.' You need to understand that and follow Jesus."

The conversation was interrupted by screams from a table across the yard. A drunk man had overturned the table and was bellowing that Annie should have been his wife. The man threw off his jacket to reveal a black tactical vest that he said was a bomb. His hand was clutching a detonator. Telling everyone to sit down and no talking, he declared that the bomb would go off if he heard sirens. Then he launched into his diatribe yelling that he had introduced Doug to Annie and Doug stole her. I was staring at Annie and praying; Mom had her head in her arms praying. When I looked over at Rob, he wasn't there. Turning to look for him, he was sitting in a chair next to the man focused on him intently. The man howled and sobbed, pacing away from Rob then toward him. When the man looked to Heaven and bellowed at God, Rob leapt up and yanked the man's thumb away from the detonator causing the man to cry out in pain. The detonator fell out of his hand, dangling on a wire. Then Rob hoisted the man on his shoulder and ran to the back of the large yard. The police department probably got twenty 911 calls at that moment. Rob then dumped him on the ground and sat on his chest.

In minutes, Police arrived and they were told what happened and pointed to where Rob was sitting. The bomb squad was called and they also arrived in minutes. With helmets and shields, they approached Rob and the man. After a while, Rob trotted toward the group who responded with cheers and whistles, and I started breathing again. Wanting so much to rush to him, I watched with a mixture of admiration and envy as he embraced Annie warmly, holding her for a long time. Doug embraced him also. Rob seemed to be making his way back to Mom and me as people gave him pats on the back and he paused to listen to them. When he got to us, he said we should make ourselves comfortable until Police were done investigating. We all had no appetite at that point and could find nothing to talk about. Rob watched the people and several stopped to say something to him. I checked with Annie to see if she needed anything then we walked into the house and I came out with coffee.

More Police arrived and they began taking statements. When Mom and my statements were recorded, they said we could go. Rob walked into the house with us to find Annie but she was in her room. Then we went to the car and he shut my door bending down to look at us through the window. Mom invited him to come over but he said he would probably be the last to leave. Reluctantly, I left him there and watched him in the rear view mirror. As we drove away, he stayed where he was with his hands in his pockets.

"It looks like he's interested, Lord," I whispered.

Chapter 6

Because Annie resigned from her position to be with her children and I never got a call back to the filing job, I lost track of Rob. Though I let God know that I missed Rob and longed for him to be in my life, Mom and I were fulfilled with prayer, Bible study, church activities and events. The events, sometimes community-wide and state-wide, were attended by Christians from many churches. At one of them, Buster, a widow, who was forty-ish, with a Santa-like appearance, including his jolly laugh and smile, was seated with Mom and me at a luncheon table. My un-shy Mom struck up a conversation with him which turned into a very interesting Bible study. At following events, we somehow managed to meet up; I don't know if it was God or Buster who was making that happen. My Mom was wishing she were twenty years younger and let me know she would be happy with him as a son-in-law.

At church one Sunday, Buster showed up, sitting next to my mom. Wanting to ignore him, Mom nudged me with her elbow and I greeted him. With sadness, I silently prayed that, though Buster would probably be an excellent husband, I could not honestly love him. Thinking of the thousands of marriages throughout history that had been arranged by parents, I sympathized with the women who were being brought men they didn't love. Jesus, I think, reminded me, in this silent conversation, that love was not an emotion but a decision. Jesus, I think, also reminded me that Rob was not a believer. With a sigh, I pulled a tissue out of my purse to dab my eyes and prayed for Rob to be born-again.

As the pastor began his message, the church door opened and a shot was fired; the pastor went down. I slipped into a crawling position along with my mom and Buster. It looked like most of the congregation did the same. The only sounds were weeping and the whispers of prayer. Thank God, most children were in a separate building.

"If I hear sirens, people die!" the man's voice bellowed. "If I hear movement, people die!"

After a minute, the man, in jeans and tee shirt, appeared at the end of the pew walking toward the pulpit with rifle raised. In another minute, another two shots rang out. The man bellowed something. Then the church door closed; someone had escaped. Silence for over a minute then a woman cried out. Was that the pastor's wife? Daring to look over the back of the bench, the shooter shoved the pastor's wife toward her husband. She cried out again with horror. The shooter stood behind her with rifle raised bellowing at her. Then the lights went out and it was pitch black because the sanctuary had no outside windows. The church door closed again; someone had escaped. Mom moved away from me and I assumed she was heading for the door. I followed but a shot rang out then another and I ducked into a pew, again in a crawling position; Mom and Buster kept going followed by the door closing.

Sirens were now approaching and I braced myself thinking the shooter would keep his promise, but the only sounds were weeping and praying. The door opened then lights came on. A line of SWAT police passed by me with rifles raised followed by a gurney pushed by medics. They rushed to the pulpit. The pastor's wife, hysterical, was escorted down the aisle followed by the pastor on the gurney. The SWAT team was huddled at the bottom of the steps to the left of the pulpit. Another gurney arrived heading toward the SWAT team then someone was rolled out of it. A different set of police arrived and asked us to remain in our seats then they began taking statements.

Mom rushed to embrace me when I finally stepped out of the church. Buster was still with her, patting my shoulder. Inviting him to Sunday dinner, we went home to enjoy her wonderful cooking. As was my custom, I announced I was taking a walk and Buster joined me.

"You probably know I came to your church to see you," Buster stated. "I'd like to spend time with you."

"I have to be honest," I said, looking at him with sadness, "I love someone else."

"Does he return your love?" Buster challenged with concern. "Where is he?"

"Has my mom been talking to you?" I retorted with irritation because I was sure she had been.

"She's concerned," Buster admitted. "He's not a believer and, well, he isn't here, is he? I'm here."

With a sigh, I turned to return to the trailer. He walked along quietly and thankfully, said 'good-bye' to my mom and left. Irritated with her, I planned to go to my room but Mom was watching a report of the shooting.

"The shooter, Mike McNamara, a thirty-year-old resident, shot and killed the pastor, Graham Masters. He was taken down by one of the congregation, Robert Burns, who was taken to General Hospital with gun shot wounds. He's in stable condition."

Grabbing my purse, I ran to my car; Mom ran after me and we raced to the hospital. Asking about Rob at the information counter, we were told he was in Emergency. Rushing to that area of the hospital, we asked about him at the window but we weren't related so they wouldn't tell us anything.

"Shelly?" asked a man from behind me.

Turning to answer, it was one of Rob's brothers.

"Steve," he said, offering his hand. "I saw you at the wedding."

"Oh," I responded brilliantly. "This is my mom, Betty."

"Yes, Betty," Steve repeated. "Rob mentions both of you often."

"How is he?" I blurted with near hysteria.

"He's fine. He's fine," Steve laughed. "Nothing stops him."

"What happened?" I pressed.

"They had to fix his leg," Steve answered.

"Fix it?" I questioned, having never heard of a wound being 'fixed'.

Steve froze for a minute as though something had become clear to him.

"Let's sit down," Steve suggested. "We'll see Rob when they're done."

An hour after we arrived, Steve said we could see Rob and he led us through the corridors and up elevators to his room. As Steve opened the door, Rob smiled immediately. Oh! How I wanted to rush into his arms!

"How's the leg?" Steve asked, standing beside Rob.

"They're making adjustments," Rob answered looking up at him then he looked at me.

"How are you?" he asked warmly and I was drawn to him finding myself standing as close to him as I could.

To me at that moment, no-one else was in the room.

"Blessed I am," I answered and my mom said 'amen'. "I heard you visited my church."

"Did you?" Rob laughed, throwing his head back like he does. "I did. I did. You know why?"

I shook my head that I didn't know why.

"I came to your church because I decided to follow Jesus," Rob explained. "I wanted to make that confession with you and your mom."

"Praise God," Mom murmured.

As tears wet my face, I looked to Heaven, and when I looked back at him, he had fear in his eyes.

"What's wrong?" I asked softly as my hand went automatically onto his shoulder to offer comfort.

He took my hand off his shoulder and held it, staring at me with apprehension.

"Would you marry a man with no legs?" he whispered with a choke.

Looking at his legs, I could now see there were no lumps in the bed where his legs should be. My mind, racing back to the tornado, the hotel, the protest, the bomber and the shooter, could not truly comprehend the reality before it.

"I would marry a man with no legs," I answered feeling like I was becoming one with him at that moment.

"Would you marry me, then?" he asked.

"I would definitely marry you," I answered, now having permission to slip an arm behind his head and an arm across his chest, kissing his temple, his cheek then his lips.

His face puckered with tears and he moved over inviting me to lay beside him. I felt like the half of me that had been missing all my life was now restored. Forehead to forehead, he told me he lost his legs in a freak accident at a military drill. He said it was the best place possible to have that kind of accident since his fellow soldiers knew how to get him where he needed to go, and he received the best possible treatment and rehabilitation. No-one around him at that time would let him remember that he had no legs. They in fact challenged him to not only test his limits but overcome them. When he left the hard-core military, his brothers took over where the soldiers left off. The only situation that scared him was marriage; he wasn't sure if he could be a proper husband and there was no way he could test himself.

"So I guess God arranged some tests, didn't he?" Rob suggested.

"Yeah, I guess he did," I agreed.

"And you, risking your life for me, joking in the face of danger, never complaining, always there for me..." he relayed bringing his face close to mine. "You..."

He kissed me and passion was rising in both of us.

"Shelly!" Mom interrupted.

Looking down at Rob's bed clothes, another lump had appeared.

"Save that for me, will you," I whispered.

"With pleasure," he promised as he caressed my lips one more time.

"Shelly!" Mom repeated.

I felt like I was ripping in half as I moved away from him and walked backward toward the door, bumping into Mom.

Rob lost no time arranging the wedding, only a month away, in the church on Parsons Road. In one of our many conversations, I asked who Lori was and he said she was his sister. Then I asked if she could help me and Mom pick out a gown and a Mother's dress; she did more than that. She helped me pick a wardrobe on Rob's credit card and took me to her makeup and hair stylist. Annie was maid of honor and Lori said she would be a bridesmaid.

To my surprise one night, I came home from the grocery store and Rob was there. He had arranged with Mom to come over for an engagement supper. Before Mom served the meal, he opened a ring box and put a stunning engagement ring on my finger. He also had a ring for me to put on his finger. When we were done eating, I said I was taking my walk, but Mom made Rob go home. She said there was too much temptation for us to be alone. She also made Rob promise he would not see me before the wedding.

The wedding ceremony was beautiful. As I walked down the aisle toward Rob, he looked like he was going to faint. Both of our eyes were teary as we said vows. When we drew close to kiss and end the ceremony, the electricity flowing between us was overpowering. As was the custom now, at the reception, Lori, Annie and I danced for the crowd. Then Rob with his brothers and some of his soldier friends brought down the house. Since that could not be topped, Rob and I threw the bouquet and garter and rushed to his waiting car.

Though he told people we were going to a resort, he drove to his house, our house, for our wedding night. He lived in a rural area surrounded by land and woods and the house was a restored brick built in the 1700's. He carried me over the threshold and walked me up the stairs to our room. Like his very first office, the walls were sculpted mahogany with matching furniture and a 1700-style bed with canopy. Wanting to savor every moment, we disrobed each other slowly to remove everything between us and continued the passion that was ignited that day in the hospital. Let me assure you, having no legs did not inhibit Rob's ability to use the tools designed by God to become one with me.

The next morning, he gave me a tour showing me parts of the house that were restored to their original condition. We walked to the barn, passing a vegetable garden, where a farm hand was caring for a couple of cows, chickens and horses and Rob promised me horse rides as often as I wanted. Hopping on an ATV, we toured the fields and the woods. We sat by a stream on a blanket discussing our future and the possibility of having children; then we enjoyed each other again.

As Rob and Mom had discussed, unknown to me of course, the trailer was sold and Mom moved into a part of the house originally designed for servants with bedrooms, bathroom and kitchen. It was the perfect setup. Because Rob had the resources, we were able to pursue the cause of my infertility and I conceived, not once, but three times. Rob and I often compared the three children to the tornado, the protestors and the shooter.

Our house became the center of family and church activity and our bedroom was our Garden of Eden. I thanked God every day, sometimes multiple times a day, that I was the one who got to love him.

In His Presence
By LK Wollett

Chapter 1

Yesterday, from my seat by the window, I watched our outdated car pull into a parking spot and he got out with a bouquet of flowers from the grocery store, even though I told him a hundred times not to spend the money. Always stubborn, he is. Though he tried to walk briskly like he did when he was seventeen, his silver-haired head leaned forward a little and I knew his arthritis was hurting. Disappearing into the front door of the nursing home, attendants and residents called his name, Patrick, and he waved, but not wavering from his destination: me, Lucy, his wife of many decades. His wife, unable to be his wife anymore, with heart and lung problems and other problems I can't begin to describe.

'How's my girl', he greeted, like every time, with a peck on my lips before he replaced last week's flowers with fresh ones. Then he sat as close to me as he could, put his arm on the back of my chair with his hand on my shoulder, that he caressed occasionally. He studied my face as he asked about doctor visits, activities and any other thing he could think of. Then he talked about his day at his wood shop with his two employees where they build tables, cabinets, and just about anything anyone can ask for. His well-known reputation keeps business coming in though it never made him rich, which is why he is still working in his early seventies.

When my meal arrived, he crooned over the meatloaf like he was jealous. Because my fingers are crooked and I can't hold utensils very well, he cut what needed to be cut offering me bites; taking some bites himself because I won't eat it all. All the while, he is making me smile or laugh. Sometimes, I laid my head on the chair to look at him and absorb his presence; it is so valuable to me. As the sun approached the horizon, he started talking about his next visit which I appreciated so much otherwise I would fall into despair at his departure. Before he disappeared, he turned and threw me a kiss.

Today, he didn't come, but my daughter, Maryann, did show up to tell me, like she was giving me a weather report, that he passed away in the night. As I stared at her in disbelief, she started asking about funeral arrangements.

"He was here yesterday like always," I interrupted. "He was fine."

"People die in their seventies, Mom," Maryann declared. "It shouldn't be a shock."

"He wasn't sick," I insisted. "What is on the coroner's report?"

"I don't know!" Maryann wailed. "How can I know that?"

"You can ask for it," I answered gently.

"AAAGGGHHH!" she growled. "I'm going to the funeral home. I tried to ask you about the arrangements - remember that!"

Maryann huffed out of the room not looking back. Almost forty, she was on her third marriage with three children, Kelly, a girl, age eighteen; Junior, age ten, and Jaye, age five. All with different fathers. I called my sister, Jenny, who lost no time sharing her problems.

"Patrick is gone," I stated when I could get a word in.

"Gone?" Jenny repeated.

"Passed away," I restated.

"No way!" Jenny blurted. "He delivered that table the other day...he was fine. He was moving things around like he was a teenager."

"I know!" I exclaimed. "He was here yesterday like always and there was no sign..."

One of the attendants said I had a visitor and I told Jenny I would call back. It was Brad, one of Patrick's employees and, unlike my daughter, he looked very upset.

"Mrs. Hayes," he greeted solemnly taking my hand. "I am so sorry. It's all a shock."

"Do you know what happened?" I asked as I directed him to a chair.

"No, Ma'am," he answered. "He left the shop yesterday like always and next thing I know, I get a call that he's dead and the shop would be closed."

"When were you called?" I asked.

"It was about ten o'clock last night," Brad replied. "I was waiting on a show to come on and got the call before it started."

"That's only three hours after I saw him," I murmured to myself. "Surely he would have mentioned something like a stomach ache or headache."

"There's those widow-makers, you know," Brad offered, trying to be helpful. "When those arteries are blocked."

"You could be right, Brad," I sighed.

"About the shop," Brad started. "I'm sorry to ask. Can I get unemployment?"

Suddenly, I realized how his life had been turned upside-down, same as mine.

"Who called you?" I responded.

"Maryann," Brad answered.

"Can you and Dave keep the shop running?" I asked and his face lit up.

"Not as good as Patrick," he replied humbly, "but sure! Yes!"

"I'll call you," I promised as I rose to get my address book and handed it to him. "Write your number in here. Either you will get unemployment or a pay check, OK?"

When Brad left, my supper tray was brought which emphasized Patrick's absence. The shock of his passing had pumped me with adrenaline which was now replaced with the ache of separation. Looking at the attendant, I said I couldn't eat and she, with tenderness, told me I had to eat something. To please her, I took a few bites until my shirt was soaked with tears and she took it away.

The next day I called the shop's accountant and he stopped by. Showing me bank statements, savings and investment accounts and the insurance policy, he said finances were in good shape plus there was no debt. My face puckered with gratitude for Patrick's good sense and discipline. Telling the accountant I wanted to keep the shop open, he thought that would be possible. The software in the shop would keep track of sales, inventory, expenses and payroll. 'Software'. I barely knew what that meant because I never got on the computer bandwagon.

When my doctor visited, I told him I wanted to move home and he, of course, advised against it but I asked him to start the process, rejecting any home health visits. This news did not please Maryann arguing with me on the phone for nearly an hour before she hung up in frustration. Since she wouldn't pick me up, I called Brad and he arrived promptly. Pulling up to my house, I had Brad help me up the porch stairs then I walked in using my walker while he brought in my things. Living room, stairs to the right, dining room ahead, office with bathroom to the right then kitchen. Nothing had changed since I left and it was clean. I knew I would need help to keep it clean; I didn't have the strength or even the will.

I wanted to go upstairs just once, then I wouldn't be able to go up anymore. Brad helped me and let me hold his arm since I didn't have my walker. Three bedrooms and a bath upstairs. Glancing at the vacant bedrooms that were once Maryann's and her brother's, Martin, I lingered in the bathroom remembering morning and evening routines with Patrick including steamy baths. Then, knowing it would hurt, I went to my bedroom. Telling Brad he could go, I lay on my side of the bed, embraced Patrick's pillow and caressed the sheets wishing I could caress his skin again and that special private place that drove him crazy. Then I laid on his side of the bed to weep myself to sleep.

The next morning, my neighbor, Andy, a widow with a couple of grown children, who was about Patrick's age, knocked on my door offering to help. Taking him up on it, I said I needed a ride to the funeral home where the funeral director, Charles, greeted us. He described Maryann's arrangements and I said I wanted to see Patrick. At my insistence, Charles gave me the address of the warehouse where Patrick was stored and Andy drove me there.

"You know," Andy began as we pulled away, "I miss Patrick, too. I don't want to let go of him either."

"If you saw him on that last day," I replied, "you would understand."

"I did see him actually," Andy continued, "talking to Maryann and her husband. Well, more like fighting."

"Not surprised they were fighting!" I said shaking my head. "Did you hear anything?"

"No, just raised voices," Andy answered.

Maryann. Always broke; always in a crises; never choosing a man who would work eight hours a day or choosing to work herself for that matter. Patrick and I discussed for hours how to help her, never arriving at a good answer.

At the warehouse, a kind lady graciously led Andy and me to Patrick.

"What are those spots on his face?" I asked.

"Petechial hemorrhages," the lady said. "Common in asphyxiation."

"Was asphyxiation the cause of death?" I questioned.

"Acute cardiac arrest is written as the cause," the lady stated looking at a computer tablet, "which can cause asphyxiation."

"There was nothing wrong with his heart," I murmured to myself as I turned to leave.

"Lucy, can I speak plainly?" Andy began as we got into the car. "If you think there is foul play, call the police."

Asking Andy for another favor, I had him drive past the shop and it was closed. Using Andy's cell phone, we called Brad.

"Brad," I asked, "Do you have a key to the shop?"

"No, Ma'am," Brad answered.

"I'm sorry about that," I responded. "I'll get you a key so you can open tomorrow. Today will be a bereavement day, ok?"

Brad was happy with that and I had Andy call Maryann.

"I want the shop to be open tomorrow," I stated firmly.

"AAAGGGHHH!" Maryann howled. "You're screwing up everything! You left the nursing home and now you want to open the shop?"

"Yes," I affirmed.

"You should let me handle this," Maryann insisted.

I didn't want to say to her that I wouldn't let her handle my garbage let alone my life, so I asked about her brother.

"Does Martin know?" I asked.

"No!," Maryann blurted with disdain. "He's always out of the country, you know, with his rich friends."

Martin, having his dad's talent, invented a tool that was sold in the shop and on the internet then the patent was bought by some corporation for a huge amount, making him financially independent.

"I want the shop to be open tomorrow," I repeated to Maryann then, when I got home, I called Martin on the land line and got his voice mail.

Chapter 2

Brad called me the next morning; he and Dave were waiting at the shop. I asked him to pick me up then we called a locksmith. Both boys went to work immediately and I sat at Patrick's desk looking in drawers when the phone rang. A customer asked about delivery of her table; the boys told me when it would be delivered and she was happy. Then Brad told me they were running out of adhesive. Asking him where to get it, he said we had to send a purchase order to the adhesive company. Asking him where the purchase orders were filed, he said they were on the computer. I had been ignoring that computer monitor on the desk with no clue how to start it let alone use it so I called Andy and he came over.

With some clicks and questions, Andy got the adhesive purchased and printed some orders from the internet. He also went through the mail, finding checks and made out a deposit slip. Asking him if he might want to work in the shop, he said he would help temporarily but I needed to hire a manager. That made sense to me and I asked the boys first; neither were interested.

Maryann came in with her children. Offering hugs, the children complied but Maryann kept her distance then she pulled me aside to tell me she needed money. This was a common occurrence that I had been spared during my stay in the nursing home. Though I wondered what it was for, I knew the question would upset her. I told her I wanted the keys to the shop so she yanked them out of her purse and thrust them at me. At the desk, I looked at the bank balance and past checks Patrick had written and I gave her the same amount he did. With 'Thanks, Mom', at least, she left.

Later that day, Charles presided at the funeral since Patrick and I had no church affiliation. Based on what Andy and I told him, Charles pieced together Patrick's life best he could. 'He was a good man; a family man; a good citizen' - everything you'd expect to hear about someone like Patrick. After the funeral, Andy, Dave, Brad, Maryann's family, and

Jenny with her husband came to the house and I had them pick up some restaurant food. It wasn't a happy gathering, I can tell you. Brad and Dave were quiet, concentrating on their food. Jenny reported all her problems. The children complained to Maryann and Tom about their promise to move to Hollywood or other issues unresolved.

"Mom?" I then heard from the living room.

Getting up from my chair and wheeling my walker toward the voice, it was Martin. Holding my arms toward him, he embraced me like I hadn't been embraced for a long time. Tears escaped as I looked up at him. His kind, light brown eyes were drinking me in, as he rubbed my shoulders saying how he just heard the message about Dad's death and rushed to get here. Returning with me to the dining room, he greeted the ones he knew then he was introduced to everyone he didn't know. Shortly after, Andy, Jenny and Husband, Maryann, Tom and the children left. Brad, Dave, and Martin had a lot to talk about and I was happy listening to them.

The next morning was Sunday and Martin was downstairs making coffee when I woke up. Just turning fifty, he was taller than his dad and had managed to stay slim, looking good in his white dress shirt and black pressed slacks. He was going to church which was not a surprise; he had gotten involved in church in high school and announced to Patrick and me that he was following Jesus. Though he often spoke of Jesus to all of us, none of us became as involved or dedicated as he was.

He invited me to go and I declined but he got me coffee and some toast before he left. Sitting on the couch, I picked up the remote but had no idea how to turn on the TV. Sitting by myself in the quiet of the room, I concluded I should have gone to church. Then someone knocked on the door. Introducing herself as Sally Rogers, real estate agent, she said she was following up on the sale of the house and the shop.

"Who told you I was selling?" I stammered.

"Your daughter," Sally answered. "Maryann."

"When was this?" I blurted with shock.

"Ahhh, Wednesday?" Sally responded now getting a little embarrassed.

"The day after his death," I murmured to myself looking away from Sally.

"What was that?" Sally asked now with a worried look.

"I'm sorry," I said, "Will you come in?"

She walked in and I offered her coffee which she poured for herself seeing it was awkward for me. Filling my coffee cup too, we sat at the dining room table. She explained that she had the house and shop appraised and gave me the substantial figure. Asking her to stay and speak to my son, I found out that she was in her late forties, divorced with grown children, all situated in their own lives.

Martin walked into the dining room and introduced himself. Also getting coffee and refilling ours, he sat with us and, at Sally's prompting, shared that he worked for a Christian organization that planted churches all over the world. He was married but lost his wife to an illness and he never pursued marriage after that. They had no children. While I admired what Martin had described, Sally shifted uncomfortably in her chair and said she had other appointments. At my request, she told Martin about Maryann's inquiry on the house and the shop.

"It's obvious, isn't it?" Martin stated sadly after Sally left. "Maryann was planning to sell the shop and house to end her money problems."

"Do you think she could have caused Patrick's death?" I ventured to ask.

"Murder?" Martin blurted with surprise, leaning back in his chair and looking to Heaven.

"Andy said Patrick was arguing with Maryann and Tom on the day he died," I offered then I remembered. "The children said something about moving to Hollywood."

"Are you hungry?" Martin asked as he rose from his chair and headed to the kitchen. "I'm hungry."

Obviously Martin thought I was over-reacting.

On Monday morning, Martin and I went to the shop where Brad and Dave were already working. Martin got me a chair and, like he had never left, he's sat at Patrick's desk, and turned on the computer. When customers came in, my walker and I greeted them, showing them catalogs and giving them business cards. Occasionally, they purchased items for sale.

Maryann came in with the children, pulled me aside and asked me for money. Walking to Martin, he wrote a check for the same amount, but notified Maryann she had to wean herself off of her dad's money. Of course she flew into a rage and Martin walked her outside the store.

"I can't believe you won't help me!" she screamed, "or the kids! You've got more than enough."

"You're not helping yourself, Maryann," Martin responded calmly. "If you had taken a job fifteen years ago, you would be in management now."

"What about a woman being a homemaker?" she argued. "Surely God wants me to stay home!"

"The same goes for your husbands," Martin retorted. "You are all like financial vampires sucking money out of other people."

"I can't live on what they give me!" Maryann sobbed, now trying tears.

"Then you have to cut back," Martin answered firmly. "Necessities only, generic brands, thrift stores..."

"AAAGGGHHH!" Maryann growled loudly as she stomped away toward her luxury, current-model car, her children following, clamoring for her attention.

Martin shook his head as he saw her light up a cigarette when she got in the car.

"She'll be back," Brad stated emphatically as Martin came into the store. "She never listened to your dad either."

"This time, we will pray and let God handle it," Martin answered and, as he said the prayer, Brad, Dave and I agreed.

The next Monday, Maryann returned with the children. Although Martin gave her a check, he also invited them to church, and Kelly, the eighteen-year-old, said she wanted to go.

For almost a year after that, Martin and I went to the shop and, every week, we picked up Kelly to go to church. Martin eventually hired Kelly to pack and ship items.

One morning, I didn't have the strength to rise up and Martin pulled me close to him.

"It might be time for me to join Patrick," I murmured. "You should call someone to come in and help."

"We can do that," Martin, letting out a deep sigh, agreed softly. "I can call Jane and Clarissa."

I nodded, snuggling against him, grateful for his closeness.

"Mom, we talked about Jesus before, remember?" Martin asked gently. "Do you believe he died for you?"

"I do believe it," I stated. "Did your dad believe? Will I see him in Heaven?"

"He would never state it like you just did," Martin answered, "so I don't know."

"But he was a good man," I offered, looking up at Martin with hope.

"Mom, you know better than that," Martin scolded pulling away from me. "It's Jesus' sacrifice that saves; not how we live."

"So a murderer can believe in Jesus and go to Heaven?" I challenged, wanting desperately to hear that Patrick was in Heaven.

"Really, Mom?" Martin retorted. "Believing in Jesus includes loving him. Anyone who believes in Jesus will not murder. They will strive to make him happy; just like you strived to make Dad happy."

That was perfectly clear to me and I said no more.

"I hope Dad is in Heaven," Martin stated, pulling me close again, "but, when you meet Jesus, nothing else will matter. Nothing else."

Chapter 3

Martin lingered by the lowered casket in the cemetery, feeling the pain of physical separation from his mother and father. Kelly stood by him, holding his hand, looking up at him with admiration. Friends from church were waiting to go to his parents' house so he tore himself away. At the house, it was comforting to have friends and family close by, but he was glad when they started cleaning up to leave. Maryann, her husband and the children stayed behind.

"We need to sell the house," Maryann stated emphatically. "And the shop. I own half of the shop now."

"The shop is making money," Martin responded with disdain. "Selling it is a mistake."

"I want half of the profit then," Maryann demanded. "I'm part owner."

"I have an appointment with the accountant," Martin sighed deeply. "You'll be getting money from insurance and when the financial accounts are closed. He'll get a check for you as soon as he can."

The next day at the shop, Martin got a call from Maryann to meet her at the house. When he got there, Sally, the real estate agent, was with her. Martin told both women that the house could not be listed until they met with the accountant. Maryann replied that Sally just wanted to record the house's features but the next day, a for sale sign was in the yard. Knowing he could fight his sister for the house, he decided to let her proceed and deal with the red tape that was bound to entangle her. But his sister's callous attitude toward her parents' deaths made him wonder if she was capable of murder and this became a nagging question. A church friend, Jason, came into his mind; he worked for the police department.

That night, as Martin slept, he was awakened by a movement in his bed. Turning over, Kelly was laying beside him in a transparent negligee. Jumping out of bed and grabbing his robe, he rushed down to the living room. She followed, standing before him, smiling, with sexually aroused supple breasts clearly visible along with the dark hair of her groin. Covering her with an afghan from back of the couch then rushing to the land line, he called Jason asking him to bring his wife.

"What are you doing here?" he finally stammered to Kelly.

"You've been so sad," Kelly answered. "I wanted to make you happy. A lot of guys say that I make them happy."

Martin's heart sank that this young girl had already experienced a 'lot of guys'.

"Don't you know that God wants you to give yourself to your husband?" Martin exclaimed. "You've been hearing that at church, haven't you?"

"I don't understand what they're saying at church," Kelly answered coyly.

"OK, I'm saying this in very plain language," Martin stated with some impatience. "Don't have sex with anyone except your husband. Did you understand that?"

"We could be married, couldn't we?" Kelly offered hopefully.

"No!" Martin exclaimed, quite exasperated. "I'm your uncle and I'm thirty years older!"

"But you're so much nicer than other guys," Kelly whined. "So much nicer than my stepdad."

"You are experiencing the love of Jesus," Martin explained. "You can experience that from a husband who is born-again."

Jason knocked on the door and Martin stepped onto the porch to explain the situation. The wife, Maria, went into Kelly and got her dressed; then they took her to their house. The next day, Jason brought Kelly to the shop and Martin blushed remembering her supple breasts.

"Are you alright?" Jason asked Martin with concern.

"A little shook up," Martin replied with an embarrassed laugh. "There is so much chaos here; planting churches in hostile countries is almost easier."

"Maybe she shouldn't work here," Jason suggested.

"Her family situation is horrible," Martin explained. "This is the only stability she has right now. I'm waiting for God to help her."

"She told Maria her family is moving to Hollywood," Jason stated. "Kelly said she wants to stay here."

The mention of Hollywood made Martin remember his mom's statement about murder and that Jason worked at the police department. Martin took Jason outside.

"My mom suspected my dad was murdered," Martin began and added his mom's reasons for the suspicion. "Can that be investigated?"

"Over a year ago, wasn't it?" Jason mused. "It's a long shot, but I'll check."

Later that day Jason got a murder case opened and Martin's house was cordoned off as a crime scene. Martin got a furnished apartment. Maryann went ballistic and charged into the shop.

"You are out of your f-ing mind!" Maryann bellowed leaning over the desk. "Dad died of natural causes!"

"Just cooperate with police and it will be over soon," Martin answered calmly, looking at Brad and Dave who were snickering.

"I'm going to stop you!" Maryann howled. "This is cruel and unusual punishment! You have brainwashed Kelly and now this!"

"Maryann," Martin said softly, standing up, taking her shoulders. "Don't waste money on lawyers. You will be hurting yourself. Let the police investigate. If Dad was murdered, you want the killer found, don't you? Anyone capable of murder will murder again."

This statement seemed to freeze Maryann for a few seconds then she turned abruptly to leave.

"When do I get money from the shop?" Maryann added before walking out the door.

"When the month closes, the profit will be split," Martin sighed sitting down again. "You should have a check by the fourth or fifth. You have to pay taxes on that, Maryann. Don't spend all of it."

She burst out of the door with her nose in the air.

"She'd have more money if she didn't spend it on that club," Brad stated casually.

"What club?" Martin asked just as casually, thinking it was a garden club or maybe a local bar.

"The X club at the edge of town," Brad answered. "It's a strip club. Kelly's been there."

"Kelly," Martin called and she came from the back room where she had been packing items for shipment.

"Have you been to the X club?" Martin asked.

"Yeah," Kelly answered hesitantly. "Why?"

"Christians don't go to X clubs," Martin instructed.

"It was my graduation party," Kelly quickly explained. "I got to pick one of the strippers as a graduation gift."

Martin took Kelly outside away from Brad and Dave who were all too interested.

"You got to pick a stripper?" Martin repeated, hoping it wasn't for the reason he was thinking.

"Yeah, for my first time," Kelly replied with a lowered voice, looking away. "I know that's wrong now."

Looking to Heaven with tears, Martin embraced her.

"Thank God you know that now, Kelly," Martin repeated. "Thank God."

Kelly explained that her mom and stepdad went to the X club regularly leaving her with the boys. Her mom and stepdad were very excited about Kelly's graduation present and so Kelly was excited as well. The stripper was a young man unknown to her and was very pleasant, patiently explaining to Kelly what he was going to do and seeming to enjoy anything that aroused Kelly. Kelly didn't know that the encounter was being televised not only in one of the club's party rooms but streamed on the internet. The video went viral in the porn world making thousands of dollars for the club and a cut went to Maryann. Kelly said her mom was already talking about Junior's graduation present. After graduation, Kelly said Maryann started hinting that Kelly could be a stripper which was making Kelly uncomfortable, so Kelly was relieved when Martin invited them to church.

"I want to stay with you, Martin," Kelly begged as tears escaped. "I feel safe with you. My mom wants me to go home and be a stripper."

"Jason, Maria and I will keep you safe for now," Martin assured her looking into her eyes. "But God is your provider. Follow Jesus, read your Bible, pray, and God will draw close to you. He will find you a husband if that's what you want or he may have plans for you that are better. Trust him."

The next day, Kelly didn't come to work so Martin called Jason. Jason said Kelly left with her parents. The day passed normally until it was time to close the shop. Kelly called Martin's cell phone.

"Martin," Kelly whispered urgently. "I'm at the strip club. Can you come and get me?"

Then the call ended. Martin didn't know what to do and he called Jason. They prayed. Martin's cell phone rang again.

"Can you come and get me?" Kelly wailed.

The call ended. Martin called Jason and Jason called his friends at the police station. They decided to meet in the parking lot of the X club which was a few miles outside city limits. With raucous music blaring through the night air, neon lights outlined the roof and sides of the club and a hundred cars were in the parking lot. Three officers walked into the club with Jason and Martin behind them. The manager greeted them immediately and they asked to see Kelly. When they were told Kelly wasn't there, they asked to see Maryann or her husband, Tom. Again, they were told neither were there. One of the officers said they would need a warrant to look for Kelly; Martin and Jason followed them to leave then Martin, seeing a fire alarm 'pull system', set it off. The officers, doing their duty, walked into the club motioning people to go outside. Sirens could be heard approaching. Upstairs were several rooms and people there were ordered to leave. Going down a back staircase, they came to the ground floor and found another staircase. Martin was not prepared for what he saw but the officer described it as a sex dungeon with specially designed benches, stocks where the head and hands were held in place, chains attached to walls, branding irons...

"Is someone there?" a trembling voice called.

"Kelly!" Martin cried as he rushed with the officer toward a room with a metal door.

"Martin!" Kelly exclaimed. "I've been praying, Martin! I've been praying!"

The officer reported to his colleagues that Kelly was locked in the basement; the manager appeared with a key and a thousand apologies. Kelly flew into Martin's arms, sobbing, trembling, barely able to stand. Having the manager open all the locked doors finding no-one else, they went outside. Although Kelly answered the officer's questions for his report, she refused to press charges. She told Martin she was afraid. Neither Martin or Jason wanted Kelly to go back to Maryann's. When Jason explained the situation to his wife, she agreed that Kelly should stay with them. When Martin expressed concern for their safety, Jason expressed trust in God to keep them safe. Jason and Kelly left.

The fire chief approached the officer to report there was no sign of fire and the firemen left. As people filed back into the building, Martin saw Maryann, her husband, Tom, and also Sally, the real estate agent. Sally was wearing a tight, light pink party dress that showed off her slim figure and her generous breasts, not noticeable in her business suits. Martin looked away, apologizing to God for lusting. In the last few years, Martin had been praying about leaving the church organization because traveling was getting hard and he missed the intimacy of a woman. Working in the shop answered part of the prayer so it remained to be seen if God would send him a wife.

At the shop the next morning, Martin was shocked to see the store windows smashed, tables turned over and adhesive poured over wood pieces. When Brad and Dave arrived, they surmised immediately the damage was retribution for rescuing Kelly but neither wanted to quit. Calling police to make a report and taking pictures of the damage, the three men began clean up.

Jason called with an update of the investigation. They had found cigarette ashes on Patrick's side of the bed along with strands of hair which they identified except for one strand. When Jason stated that it wasn't enough to bring in Maryann, Martin suggested they visit Sally.

The rest of the week passed without incident. Jason reported that they did visit Sally and she was extremely nervous. Asking Jason if he was done with the house, the police tape was removed and Martin arranged to meet Sally there.

"I saw you at the X club," Martin announced as soon as Sally walked into the house.

"That's my business," Sally responded defiantly.

"It's God's business," Martin answered firmly. "I'm here to tell you that God doesn't like it."

"I don't need your preaching," Sally retorted just as firmly and turned to go.

"If you helped Maryann kill my dad, you're an accomplice," Martin challenged boldly.

"I didn't help her!" Sally bellowed, twisting abruptly to face him.

"Were you aware of their plans?" Martin guessed.

"People talk and brag," Sally explained nervously. "You never know if they are serious."

"If you overheard them talking about killing my dad, you need to tell police," Martin advised.

"You need to stay out of it," Sally countered fiercely. "You don't know who you're dealing with."

"It doesn't matter," Martin declared. "No-one is bigger or badder than God."

Sally left and Martin reported to Jason what Sally said; Jason said he would follow-up with her. Then, Martin had an overwhelming desire to pray for Sally's salvation. He knelt beside the couch and, with tears, begged God to have mercy on her.

Chapter 4

Sally rushed away from Martin and, in the car, called Maryann.

"You've done it now, Girl!" Sally exclaimed. "Police are asking me about Patrick's death. Were you involved?"

"Hell, no!" Maryann yelled. "This is Martin's doing. It's all about the money."

"I'm not going down for you or anybody," Sally declared, recognizing that her long-time friend was lying. "Don't count on me for an alibi. Don't count on me for anything related to murder."

Sally recalled the number of times over the years that she and Maryann had covered for each other. She and Maryann were high school friends and they were those 'bad' girls every high school has. Both their parents let them go to a local skating rink and from there they were taken to parties. Older men at the parties lavished attention on the young girls both giving away their virginity early on. Sally and Maryann spent hours recounting to each other their sexual escapades with various partners. Because Maryann had threesome and even foursome encounters, Sally considered Maryann more advanced. Sally wasn't sure what held her back from being as brave as Maryann.

Eventually, one of the men became smitten with Sally and accepting his marriage proposal, they lived happily for several years, having two children. When the X club opened, she and her husband became regular patrons. Sally believed that the free sex environment was a stimulant for intimate relations with her husband, making them happier and closer. However, a rift occurred between them when she would not go to the sex dungeon because it was expensive to get in and she was not comfortable with that much 'freedom'. It became an obsession for her husband and he started going to the club without her. Eventually, he asked for a divorce so he could marry someone else.

Sally was smart enough and bold enough to get the house and plenty of child support in the divorce settlement. She got her real estate license and was able to work from home and when the children were in school. Her children were pre-teen and she made sure she knew where they were every minute of the day and night. Though she had to endure many heated arguments with them, she remained firm and was gratified when both of them graduated from high school, got jobs and got married.

After that, in the empty house alone, she ventured again to the X club looking for company and also real estate prospects where she met up with Maryann and Tom. She enjoyed socializing with Maryann and Tom when they were just drinking but eventually they would offer her party drugs then they would go to the sex dungeon. Maryann claimed she was just a spectator but Tom chose rough, sadistic partners. When Sally wondered about cuts and bruising, Tom said they were expert at inflicting pain with no outward effects.

During one of their socializing sessions at the X club, Maryann was raging about her financial problems saying that her dad had plenty of money but he wouldn't share. Tom, with several drinks in him, fantasized about the money they would get from sale of Patrick's house and shop. Then they started talking about crime shows that recounted investigation of murders pointing out where they would have committed the crime differently. Sally thought nothing was unusual about this conversation; crime shows were just entertainment, were they not?

At Kelly's graduation party, Sally happily went along with the 'gift' of a stripper, feeling envious even. Kelly was escorted upstairs by her choice amid cheers and whistles. When it was then announced that Kelly's encounter was going to be televised in a party room at an expensive price, the party room filled up immediately. Before Maryann and Tom left the table, Maryann asked Sally to cross her fingers for a zillion views bragging they would receive a cut. Though Sally did not join them, she found out later that Maryann received a substantial amount of money and Sally was actually happy that this would help Maryann with her financial problems.

Now, alone in her house, believing that Maryann was involved in Patrick's death, she sat at the kitchen table, looking out the sliding glass door to her back yard, remembering the many occasions celebrated there with her children. She wanted to relive those years. Though the X club came to her mind, she rejected the idea of going because she planned to stay away from Maryann. Her cell phone rang; it was Jason. Rolling her eyes, she told him they could come over and he showed up with a female officer. Sally led them to the kitchen table and offered them refreshments which they declined.

"The investigation of Patrick's house is finished," Jason began. "We found cigarette ashes in Patrick's bed and strands of hair we can't identify. Were you ever in Patrick's bedroom?"

"No!" Sally blurted. "What a ridiculous question! Why are you harassing me about this?"

"You and Maryann are friends, aren't you?" Jason answered. "You go to the X club with her."

"I go to the X club which is not against the law," Sally affirmed. "Maryann and Tom are there and we talk. That's all."

"Did they ever talk about killing Patrick?" Jason pressed.

Sally shifted and wondered if she needed a lawyer but decided against it.

"They were high; they were joking," Sally replied. "Money is a problem for them and they fantasized about selling Patrick's house and shop. The liquor was talking, not them."

"Maryann received a substantial amount of money from the X club," Jason continued and Sally interrupted him.

"Yes, from Kelly's graduation," Sally explained then she went on to describe Kelly's graduation gift.

To many people, Sally's description of Kelly's gift would have been shocking and even distressing. Jason and the officer, however, were aware of human depravity and this was a relatively mild incident.

"A large portion of that money was withdrawn as cash shortly after," Jason stated. "Do you know why?"

"How would I know that?" Sally exclaimed, quite upset. "I told you. We socialize, that's all. I'm not involved in their private life."

"Sally," Jason said seriously. "Maryann may have paid to have Patrick killed. If she did, she's a danger to everyone in her life. Think of her children."

Wanting to leave their presence, she stood up and looked out the sliding glass door.

"You can help them," Jason continued. "We need one of her cigarettes. We might be able to match the ashes found in Patrick's bedroom."

A war was raging inside Sally as she fought off the truth: helping them was the right thing to do.

"We can make this hard for you," Jason relayed. "We can get a search warrant; we can bring you in to review suspects at lineups; we can..."

"Alright!" Sally bellowed. "I can get a cigarette at the club. I'll go tonight."

When they left, Sally checked her phone and made appointments for the next few days to show houses. Looking in the fridge for something to eat, she decided she wasn't hungry and poured a glass of wine, then another. Then she showered and put on her pink party dress. Looking in the mirror, she was gratified at her slim figure and her still firm breasts, realizing that age would soon rob her of those attributes.

At the club, she ordered a drink and was relieved when Maryann and Tom joined her. Like before, they drank, swallowed their drugs, then left for the sex dungeon. Pulling out an evidence bag and writing on it the date and time as Jason had instructed, Sally discreetly dropped in the cigarette butts left by Maryann and Tom. She was about to leave when a man sat as close to her as he could, putting his arm on the back of her chair. He was probably in his forties with muscles, created by regular workouts, showing through his tight black tee shirt. His blond hair was in a ponytail.

"Sally, isn't it?" the man asked then continued. "I know Tom and he's mentioned you often."

"Yeah," Sally smiled coyly. "I've seen you around. Don't you strip sometimes?"

"Sometimes," the man answered with a smile then moving his head close to her. "I need a lot of incentive to do that. I'm very shy about showing off in front of people. I prefer private engagements. Want a drink?"

The man ordered drinks and leaned forward on his folded arms. Sally did the same.

"Rusty," he said, then with his hand under the table, he caressed Sally's breast. She inhaled involuntarily at his touch and closed her eyes.

"You don't have a man right now, do you?" Rusty murmured leaning his head close. "Tom told me you are alone. A woman like you shouldn't be alone. It's such a waste."

"The young ones get all the attention," Sally explained with a embarrassed chuckle, "which is understandable. I can see why men prefer them."

"Ahhh, but the experience," Rusty hummed. "You know some things they don't know."

The drinks arrived and Sally took a long sip, wondering where this was going.

"I can get you into the playhouse," Rusty offered. "For free. It's a different world down there."

"Thanks but that's not for me," Sally answered, shaking her head with a soft laugh. "I also prefer private engagements."

"We can go upstairs," Rusty suggested softly. "My treat."

"Listen, I have a nice house and a full fridge, not far from here," Sally finally offered and he followed her out the door.

They drove separately and Sally waited for him in the drive way as he got out of his car. He walked in before her as she locked the door. When she turned to him, he immediately kissed her passionately as he unzipped her dress to let it fall to the floor. Removing her bra, he caressed her breasts with his lips as he explored her body with his fingers lingering in her private place. As she trembled with excitement, she pulled off his tee shirt and pulled down his jeans with briefs. Spending time giving his swollen organ some attention she knew he would like, he moaned with ecstasy, murmuring that she knew how to love him. Then he laid her back, removed her panties and pushed himself inside her. When he withdrew, they both commented on the extreme ecstasy of the encounter. He said it was because she knew how to love him.

Sally then rose and asked if he was hungry. She offered hamburgers and he readily agreed. While she cooked, they asked each other 'get acquainted' questions and, after eating, she led him to her bedroom where they found a movie, during which, he engaged her again. This time, she drifted to sleep in his arms and was awakened by him, fully dressed ready to leave. He leaned down as though he was going to kiss her and put a knife to her throat.

"If you talk to the police again, I'll be back," Rusty threatened softly.

Then he ran the point of the knife on her breast creating a cut about an inch long and left. Sally grabbed a tissue to stop the bleeding and lay in the bed, catatonic. Then, panicked that she would not be able to stop the police from talking to her, Martin came to her mind and she called his cell.

"What's wrong!" Martin exclaimed, hearing panic in her voice and raising out of bed.

Starting with Jason's visit and his request for one of Maryann's cigarettes, Sally told him honestly about her encounter with Rusty and the cut of his knife. She found herself being embarrassed talking to Martin, which was unusual. Most of the time, she bragged about her sexual freedom with defiance, defending it against anyone who disagreed.

"We need to get those cigarettes to Jason," Martin stated. "You can meet Maryann at dad's house. Tell her you have additional questions about selling it. Put the evidence bag in a drawer somewhere and call me. Jason can pick it up. Is there any place you can go to - leave town?"

"My daughter, but I have appointments," Sally wailed.

"Surely someone can keep those for you!" Martin exclaimed. "I want you to leave!"

Sally said she would leave if she could. Martin's emphatic plea was a surprise to himself. Was he getting invested in Sally? A God-less woman who would be labeled a 'hoar' in many circles? He rose and went to the shop, anxious to get Sally's call. When Kelly, Brad and Dave came in, Martin got a premonition about their safety. Talking over the situation with them, they agreed that the shop should be closed. Both Brad and Dave had places they could travel to. Martin issued them pay checks with a bonus to cover travel expenses. A 'closed' sign was placed in front of operating hours in the store window. The boys worked to finish and deliver pending orders; Kelly packaged everything to be shipped. Martin called customers who had placed orders on the internet telling them the shop would be closed until further notice; he then entered an announcement on the website. Sally called saying the evidence bag was in a kitchen drawer and that she was leaving to stay with her daughter. When Martin expressed concern about Kelly, Sally offered to take her. Assuming Sally's house was being watched, Martin arranged to meet Sally outside of town. When all orders were filled, Martin drove Kelly to Jason's to get Kelly's clothes then to the meeting point. Seeing Sally waiting outside her car, Martin found himself rushing to her and had to stop himself from embracing her. Noticing Martin's concern made Sally feel something she had never felt before: a sweet, warm presence that she was drawn to. When Kelly got into the car, it made Sally sad that she had to leave Martin.

Chapter 5

Melissa, Sally's daughter, greeted her cheerfully, happy for the visit and welcomed Kelly. Melissa's husband traveled for his job so he wasn't home and they as yet had no children. As Melissa asked 'catch up' and 'get acquainted' questions, both Sally and Kelly found it difficult to respond. Neither wanted to share why they had left their town. Sally then got concerned about Melissa being left alone while her husband traveled. When Melissa got a phone call and stepped out of the room, Sally suggested to Kelly they go elsewhere; Kelly agreed readily. Pulling out her phone, Sally looked up a nearby attraction and, when Melissa came back, Sally said she and Kelly had decided to leave. Though Melissa was surprised, she offered them supper which they accepted.

On the road, Sally had Kelly look up hotels. As Kelly read the choices, Sally picked one she liked then Kelly made a reservation. In the hotel room, they put on their sleepwear and looked for a movie. Sally was slightly unnerved that Kelly wanted a movie for general audiences; they are hard to find these days and not very entertaining.

"Is PG OK?" Sally asked with frustration after searching for several minutes.

"Can I look?" Kelly offered sensing Sally's discomfort. "Here! This is PG-13 but it's about Jesus. Is this OK?"

"Yeah. Sure," Sally agreed wanting to roll her eyes, wondering how this could be a daughter of Maryann's.

The movie was several years old and, in the opening scene, the angel Gabriel informed Mary about Jesus' conception[8] and another angel instructed Joseph to take Mary as his wife[9]. Then came the nativity scene and the angels announcing the birth of Jesus to the shepherds[10].

"Do you believe this is real?" Sally asked with concern.

"I do," Kelly answered flatly. "How could it not be?"

"What do you mean?" Sally challenged.

"If God isn't real, then everything came from nothing," Kelly explained. "I don't believe that. If God created everything, then it's easy to believe he created the Bible for us and the Bible tells us what Jesus did for us."

Sally didn't pursue the conversation and looked at her phone while Kelly watched the movie, but Sally's eyes would not ignore the scenes where Jesus was flogged, mocked by soldiers and given a crown of thorns. Then Jesus, barely able to walk, carried the cross up the hill and was laid on it. Sally closed her eyes and winced as the nails were pounded into Jesus' flesh.[11] It was a huge relief when the resurrected Jesus greeted Mary. The narrator then went on to say that Jesus met with his disciples and then the movie, showing Jesus ascending into Heaven, promised that Jesus would return[12].

The next morning, Sally and Kelly spent the day at the attraction stopping for supper and returning to the hotel ready for sleep. Looking on her phone for something to do tomorrow and giving suggestions to Kelly, Kelly asked if she could find a church for Sunday service. Sally said there were plenty of churches, but which one. Kelly called Martin, telling him where they were and why they were not at Melissa's. Sally jealously listened to Kelly's soft tone with Martin and the frequent giggles. When Martin gave Kelly a church name, Sally found it on her phone and Martin hung up. There was a twinge of disappointment in Sally's heart that he did not ask for her.

In the medium size church, Kelly and Sally stood out like two aliens but people went out of their way to greet them. Kelly did all the talking, smiling and laughing while Sally listened and nodded. After some singing and announcements, the pastor gave the scripture reference, John chapter 8, 'the woman caught in adultery'. Sally's mind drifted to when she gave her virginity to someone she didn't remember. Then the rest of her lovers passed by like a parade, some with faces and some not. Rusty was last, standing before her with his knife in his hand then Martin stood beside him. Sally could see, for the first time in her life, the difference between sexual ecstasy and love. Trying to dismiss her thoughts by concentrating on her phone, her ears would not ignore verse 10 coming from the pulpit, "Woman, where are those thine accusers? hath no man condemned thee?" Then verse 11, "Neither do I condemn thee: go, and sin no more."

The words 'go, and sin no more' entered her ear as though it were alive and it traveled through her arteries into the pit of her black, cavernous, spirit-starved soul. Something ignited and she wept. Kelly knew exactly what was happening and put her arm on Sally's shoulder, drawing her close.

"You met Jesus, didn't you," Kelly whispered. "You met Jesus."

"Yes," Sally sobbed nodding, searching for a tissue. "He told me to sin no more."

"Praise God," Kelly exclaimed as quietly as she could.

"Praise God," repeated a lady and man in front of them who had turned around.

When the pastor invited people to accept the invitation to follow Jesus, Kelly encouraged Sally to go up; Kelly went with her, along with the lady and the man. Sally explained with more tears what happened and the pastor invited her to be baptized. With Kelly's encouragement, Sally accepted and the pastor said he would meet her at a creek close by. Half of the church members were waiting for her and cheered when she came out of the water. Someone put a blanket around her.

At the hotel, Sally took a shower then suggested to Kelly that they go home. Kelly was all for it. Dropping off Kelly at Jason's, Sally returned to her house. Jason called her.

"I'm surprised your back!" Jason exclaimed. "What happened?"

"I'm following Jesus," Sally answered with an open smile.

"Praise God!" Jason cheered, asked some questions then returned to the reason for his call. "Rusty slept in your bed, correct?"

"He did, I'm so sorry to admit," Sally responded with an embarrassed laugh, looking to Heaven.

"Hey! No worries! All behind you now, right?" Jason replied then requested. "I want to bag the pillows and bed clothes, OK? I have a feeling his hair will match that orphan strand."

"Ok, I'll be here," Sally stated, happy to dispose of that memory.

"Don't touch anything," Jason warned. "Detectives are coming with me. We'll take pictures and get everything bagged properly."

As Jason expected, Rusty's hair strands on Sally's bed matched the strands found in Patrick's room but it wasn't that evidence that got Rusty convicted; it was Tom's and Maryann's confessions and plea deal. In addition DNA from sperm was lifted from the bedclothes which linked Rusty to other murders. He was eventually sentenced to multiple life imprisonments; Maryann and Tom were sentenced to twenty years instead of life.

Maryann, who received monthly checks from profit of the shop, accumulated money for the first time in her life. Maryann would be nearly sixty years old and financially stable when she got out of prison. Martin visited her regularly with her boys to try to make them spiritually stable too.

Kelly married Brad who chose to follow Jesus and they had three children.

It took a while, but Sally and Martin got together. Out of embarrassment, Sally chose not to attend Martin's church. Martin, believing God was leading him to Sally, wanted to be very sure, so he made no effort to contact her. Their meeting occurred at a wedding where he was a groomsman and she was a bridesmaid and, somehow, they were paired to walk out of the church together, eat together and dance together. As they danced, Martin could feel God's love pouring through his being toward her and Sally could feel the warmth of God's love embracing her. Though they chatted a little, the real communication was in their eyes, their smiles and the blush of their cheeks.

Martin and Sally lived in his parents' house and took in Maryann's boys which was not easy. The boys were spoiled, secular and as stubborn as Maryann. With God's help though, they got through high school and Martin let them work in the shop after they graduated. As the boys matured, they began to see how Martin's choices were different from Maryann's and how Martin's choices were beneficial in the long run. They did not become financial vampires and it is unknown at this time if they have decided to follow Jesus.

Now, Sally, whenever she can, advises men and women to stay out of the X-world and live instead in the joy, peace and fulfillment of God's presence.

---

[1] John 3:3 KJV "Jesus answered and said unto him (Nicodemus), Verily, verily, I say unto thee, Except a man be born again, he cannot see the kingdom of God."

[2] Ephesians 2:8 KJV "For by grace are ye saved through faith; and that not of yourselves: it is the gift of God:..."

[3] Romans 5:5 KJV "...because the love of God is shed abroad in our hearts by the Holy Ghost (Spirit)..."

[4] Song of Solomon, a book in the Bible, is a poem about the love of a husband and wife.

[5] 1 Corinthians 6:9-10 KJV "Do you not know that the unrighteous will not inherit the kingdom of God? Do not be deceived. Neither fornicators, nor idolaters, nor adulterers, nor homosexuals, ...will inherit the kingdom of God."

[6] Revelation 20:12 KJV "And I saw the dead, small and great, stand before God; and the books were opened: and another book was opened, which is the book of life: and the dead were judged out of those things which were written in the books, according to their works."

[7] 2 Corinthians 6:14 KJV "Be ye not unequally yoked together with unbelievers..."

[8] Luke 1:26-38

[9] Matthew 1:18-25

[10] Luke 2:8-10

[11] John 19

[12] John 20-21, Acts 1